THE DEEP END

ROBERT SWINDELLS

Barrington Stoke

First published in 2013 in Great Britain by
Barrington Stoke Ltd
18 Walker Street, Edinburgh, EH3 7LP

www.barringtonstoke.co.uk

ISBN: 978-1-78112-189-4

Printed in China by Leo

Contents

Chapter 1
No One Remembered

"Hey, Sealie."

Jake Seal turned to see Tim Gittins leering at him.

"Our Matt don't half fancy your sister," he growled. "Says he's going out with her Friday night."

Jake snorted. "Asked her, has he?"

"Not yet. He's gonna do it at morning break, or lunch."

"He's got no chance," Jake told him. "Our Lisa trains Friday nights."

"Well, he'll take her out Saturday then."

"She trains Saturdays as well," Jake said. "She trains *every* night. And anyway she's got a boyfriend."

"What?" Tim hooted. "That scruffy weirdo with the bike? Our Matt's cooler than him any day."

Jake shook his head. "Rick isn't a weirdo. He's got a job, which is more than your Matt can say. And the bike's a Harley, in case you hadn't noticed. Rick is cool, Gittins, and Matt's a loser. Which makes two losers at your house."

Tim sneered. "You Seals think you're something don't you? Just because your Lisa's won a few swimming cups. Anyone can win cups if all they do is train all the time. *I* could."

"Yeah but that's the thing, isn't it?" Jake snapped. "You would never put the time in, or the effort. You don't win cups by dossing on your bed smoking. If there was a National Waste of Space Championship, I suppose you might have a chance. In fact there'd be so many cups at your place there'd be no room for your family."

When Tim balled his fists and stepped towards him, Jake knew he'd gone too far. He got set to defend himself, but just then Mr Ball the P.E. teacher came marching across the yard and stood between them.

"If you want to fight," he growled, "fight me."

"Er ... no thank you, Sir," Jake stammered. Mr Ball was six foot of hard muscle.

Mr Ball glared at Tim. "How about you, Gittins?"

"No, Sir. I was just going to shake hands with Seal."

The teacher smiled. "You'd better do it then, hadn't you? The bell's about to go any second."

The boys shook hands as the bell went to mark the start of another week at Barton Academy School.

*

Swimming trainer Marie Docker had muscles too. A hundred lengths was nothing to her –

she'd swum the English Channel a few years back. Lisa Seal arrived with her at the school gate as the bell sounded. They'd made it just in time from South Street Baths.

"You weren't bad this morning," Marie said. "If you stay focused, I reckon we could start thinking about the next Olympics."

"*Olympics?*" Lisa gulped. "*Me?*"

Marie nodded. "Sure, why not? You're the fastest free-style swimmer in the country – the fastest in *Europe*. Only that American, Silverman, and a couple of Aussies have swum faster than you this year, and Silverman'll be over the hill in four years' time. You've got as good a chance as anyone, if you train hard enough from today on."

"There's one snag," Lisa murmured. "We start working for A-levels this month."

Marie nodded. "I know, and A-levels matter." She pulled a face. "I blew mine – my mind was all on the swimming. I was going to be a vet. Now I work in a sports shop all day and coach you dawn and dusk. Believe me, Lisa, you need to get those exams."

Lisa grinned. "No pressure there then, hey?"

Marie squeezed her arm as they parted. "You can do it, love, I know you can."

Lisa swung her bag as she walked across the yard, headed for Miss Taylor's room. The other kids had gone inside already.

Miss Taylor was ready with her usual crack about Lisa's lateness. "Good afternoon, Miss Seal," she snapped. "Good of you to join us."

The other kids snickered.

"Yeah, whatever," Lisa murmured as she walked to her place. Her hair was still damp from the Baths.

"Did you say something, Lisa?" Miss Taylor asked.

"No, Miss." Lisa felt like asking what Miss Taylor had been doing at 6am when Lisa had started training, but she didn't. Old Taylor knew fine well that Lisa was already thrashing up and down the pool when she and most other people were turning over in bed for a last doze. She knew Lisa would be back there after school, too, powering up and down again while Taylor put her feet up with a cup of tea.

‘Let the sad old cow have her bit of fun,’ Lisa thought. ‘She’ll be cheering with all the rest when they parade me through Barton with my Olympic gold medal. “I used to teach her,” she’ll say, to anyone who’ll listen.’

‘Just got to bag those A-levels first ...’

*

As Jake and Lisa Seal started their school day, Councillor Farley Topham called a meeting at Barton Town Hall. The Council had been told it had to find ways of saving money. There was no way to do this without cutting back on something the town needed or enjoyed. Whatever the Council decided to cut, someone would be angry and upset. Farley Topham didn’t like it. It was no fun, upsetting people. But the orders had come from the Government – there was no money and something had to go.

“What about the swimming baths?” Topham asked the other Councillors. “South Street Baths cost thousands to run, and they’re not used as much as they once were. They’re old-fashioned, and people drive to Leeds to use the pools there.

I don't think there'd be much of a fuss if we closed them down."

Most of the Councillors thought this was a good idea. A vote was taken, and the fate of the Baths was sealed. No Councillor thought about Lisa Seal. The girl had put Barton on the map with her swimming cups and trophies, but no one remembered that South Street Baths was where she trained. No one remembered that she swam in the very early mornings, and when the South Street Baths closed, the nearest pool would be over thirty miles away.

Chapter 2
Shake Their Windows

Wednesday tea at the Seals was always fish and chips from the shop. It was Jake's favourite. Lisa always grumbled. "I'm in training, Mum. Fish and chips isn't the perfect diet for an athlete."

"Listen, love," said Grandad, who lived with them. "When I was a lad there was this runner, Alf Tupper, who won every title going. But he was useless if he didn't get his fish and chips every day."

"Yes, Grandad," Lisa sighed, "but Alf Tupper wasn't *real*, was he? He was a story in a comic."

"Not a comic, love," Grandad said. "It was the *Rover*, a boys' paper."

"The stuff in it wasn't true though, was it? It was stories."

Grandad snorted. "It was as true as the rubbish they print in the papers nowadays. And anyway fish live in water, so eating fish has got to be good for a swimmer, hasn't it?"

"Pass us the vinegar, Sis," said Jake, before Lisa could come back at Grandad. "Has Matt Gittins said anything to you yet?"

Lisa passed the bottle over. "What you on about, Jake? Why should Matt Gittins say anything to me?"

Jake grinned. "Tim told me Matt fancies you. On Monday he was going to ask you to go out with him."

"Matt *Gittins*?" Lisa stabbed a chip with her fork. "I wouldn't go out with Matt Gittins if he was the last guy in Barton."

"Lisa's *got* a boyfriend," Mum put in. "And even *he* hardly ever sees her, she's down those baths so much." She smiled at Lisa. "How did it go this afternoon, love?"

Lisa pulled a face. "OK, I suppose. Marie reckons I might qualify for the next Olympics."

Everyone stopped chewing.

"The *Olympics?*" Dad spluttered through a mouthful of cod.

Lisa nodded. "That's what she said. I've got to stay focused, that's all." She sighed. "The snag is my A-levels. I've to focus on *them* as well, and I don't know if I can focus on the two things at the same time."

Dad shook his head. "You *can't*, love, and I think you should focus on ..."

"Marie reckons I can do both," Lisa said, as fast as she could. She knew what Dad was about to say, but she couldn't imagine passing up the chance of swimming for her country.

"Marie didn't manage both, did she?" Mum chipped in. "She won silver, but that didn't get her to university. She works in a shop."

Lisa nodded. "I know, she says that herself. But I'm not chucking in swimming after all the hard work she's done with me."

Before anyone could say anything different, Rick walked in without knocking.

"Feeding time for the Seals, I see," he grinned. Here, I picked this off the mat." He put the paper down next to Mr Seal's plate and smiled at Lisa.

"Caught you on dry land for once! Fancy a burn-up?" That was Rick's term for a fast bike ride.

Lisa nodded. "Course, soon as I finish these chips."

"Give us one." Rick stuffed a chip into his cheek and winked at Jake.

Dad's voice exploded behind his paper. "Hey – they can't do that!" He lowered the paper and gazed round the table. "They're closing South Street Baths."

"Who?" asked Mum.

"The flipping *Council*. Another of their money-saving scams."

The colour left Lisa's cheeks. "What about my training?" she wailed. "Where am I supposed to swim? In my *coffee*?"

Rick laid a hand on her arm. "It'll never happen, sweetheart, we won't let it." He frowned. "Wonder what they're gonna spend the dosh on instead? Never tell us *that*, do they?"

Dad looked at Lisa. "The next nearest pool's Leeds, so that's thirty miles, give or take. Say just under an hour by car on a good day. An hour or so in the water, an hour back. Four hours in total. If you started at six, you wouldn't be back by nine. That's too late for school."

Lisa pulled a face. "I have to dry off and get dressed, and it's rush hour on the roads. There'd be ice sometimes, and snow." She shook her head. "It's too much. I can't do that day after day."

"Back in the 60s," said Grandad, "students used to *occupy* buildings to stop 'em being closed. 'Sit-ins', they were called. Or sometimes 'die-ins' or 'teach-ins'."

Dad looked at him. "Did it work, Dad?"

"Sometimes. Made the powers-that-be *listen*, see? And even when it didn't work, it was fun."

Mum shook her head. "It's a different world now, Dad. The Council would probably bulldoze the place with the protestors inside."

"Still," put in Rick, "your grandad's on the right track. Action's what's needed, not words. It's no use emailing the Council to tell them how upset you are. They get off on upsetting people. No, something's got to be done. Something that'll show them we're not about to roll over and play dead. Something that'll get us in the papers, on telly."

"OK," said Lisa, "but *what?*"

Rick looked thoughtful. "Leave it with me," he said. "I'll talk to a few people. People who've organised actions before. We should be able to come up with something that'll shake their windows a bit."

"Can *I* be in it, Rick?" Jake begged.

"Well ..." Rick looked at their dad.

"I don't think so," Dad said. "What Rick has in mind is a protest, and protests have a way of getting out of hand. A kid could get hurt – just look at what happened in London that time. What you *could* do, Jake, is write a letter to the

Council in support of your sister. Tell them how hard she trains, write about some of her trophies. Tell them you're proud of her, and say they should be proud too."

Jake pulled a face. "It isn't *cool* Dad, writing letters."

"It's a good idea, mate," said Rick. "The 'shame factor', it's called. It gets to them. In fact, it could do as much good as a march."

"Oh, all right." Jake shrugged. 'But I'll join the protest as well,' he thought. 'Just try and stop me!'

Chapter 3
No Aggro, No Coppers

Most Saturday mornings, Jake met a bunch of his mates down the Shopping Centre. The security guards there didn't like the kids who hung about, especially not kids in hooded tops. They weren't allowed to chuck you out, but they'd watch you. You were OK as long as you kept moving, but the guards would shadow you. If two or three of you stopped to check out a shop window, they'd pounce.

"What's your game?" they'd growl. "This is a shopping centre, not the flippin' park. Move on, unless you want us to call for backup."

So you'd move on, but only round the corner, or out one door and back in another. They were dead easy to wind up, those guys. And it was a laugh the way some of the shoppers edged away, like you were aliens from another planet.

The only way to be in the Shopping Centre and not have to keep moving was to get a table at BB's and sit with drinks. This was where Jake found his mates that morning. He got a Coke and joined them.

"Thought you weren't coming," his mate Minty said.

Jake looked at his watch. "It's only 9.20, you div. Anyway, listen. They're shutting South Street Baths."

They all looked at him.

"That's old news," Willie said. "And so what, anyway?"

"Our Lisa trains there."

Garfield shrugged. "Stuff happens, Jake. Get over it."

Jake shook his head. "It doesn't just happen, people *make* it happen. Which means other people can make it *un*happen."

"*Un*happen?" Minty chuckled. "Didn't learn *that* word from old Fletch, I bet." Mr Fletcher was the English teacher at the Academy.

"I got it from Lisa's boyfriend," Jake told him. "Rick Coldwell. He's getting some guys together to organise a march on the Town Hall. A protest. Cool thing to be in on, or what?"

"When?" Willie asked.

Jake shrugged. "Dunno. Soon, though. Rick says the more people take part, the better. Are you guys up for it?"

Willie grinned. "Why not? It's time *summat* happened in this dump."

The other two nodded. "Bring it on, Jake, we're in."

*

Jake didn't say anything to his mates about the letter.

First of all, he'd been all for using Facebook, or at least email, but Rick had shaken his head. "Councils don't do Facebook," he'd said, "and they'll be up to their eyes in emails. Yours would just get lost. It's got to be a letter. Send a copy to the *Times* as well, and tell Coucillor Topham you've done it." He grinned. "He can't ignore it then, see?"

Jake wrote the letter that afternoon, in his room. This is what he put:

Dear Councillor Topham,

My name is Jake Seal. I'm writing to you because my sister is Lisa Seal, the champion swimmer. I read how you are going to close the South Street Baths. Our Lisa trains there every morning and after school. She's won loads of medals and trophies and stuff. Barton's famous because of her. What's she supposed to do now? The nearest pool is thirty miles away. She'd have to get up at four every morning, and not get home till late at night. Is this the way to treat a hard-working girl who's put Barton on the map? Why not close some of those posh new Council offices and keep the Baths open?

P.S. I've sent a copy of this to the Barton Times.

Yours sincerely,

Jake Seal

He posted it in the box up the road. It would sit there till the collection on Monday, so Tuesday was the earliest it'd get to the Town Hall. Two flipping days. Three really, when an email would be there in about a second. 'No wonder it's called snail-mail,' he thought.

*

At the Gittins' house, there were no chats over fish and chips. Meals weren't a family affair over there. Tim and Matt's mum said her husband and her sons weren't paralysed, were they, and there was usually something in the fridge, so they could get their own.

On Monday night, there was an open tin of corned beef. Matt slapped three slices on a plate, dolloped them with ketchup and carried them to a chair in front of the TV. Tim was slumped on the sticky sofa, scoffing a packet of Monster Munch.

"So your stuck-up mate Jake reckons Lisa and her weirdo boyfriend are planning a protest about the Baths closing, that right?" Matt asked Tim.

Tim nodded, his eyes glued to the TV. "That's what he said at school today."

"Marching through town?"

"Something like that," said Tim,

"Do you know when?"

"No, it's not fixed yet."

"Well, keep your ears open, and let me know the minute you hear."

Tim upended his crisps and shook the last crumbs into his gaping mouth. He screwed up the packet and bowled it at a corner of the room. "Why? You thinking of joining in or summat?"

His big brother leered. "In a way, bro ... See – there's protests and there's protests. Some are peaceful, some aren't. Rick the biker, he'll want to keep it peaceful. No aggro, no coppers. I'm gonna make sure he gets the other sort." He smiled. “Wouldn’t surprise me if old Rick ends up getting his collar felt. Him *and* that stuck-up Lisa. They don’t pin Olympic medals on jailbirds, you know.”

Chapter 4
To Skin a Cat

"What I don't understand," growled a Councillor with freckles and ginger hair, "is why we're keeping the Baths open till Christmas. That's three months. Three months will cost us £45,000. If we're going to close the damn place, why not do it *now* and save the forty-five grand?"

Councillor Topham shook his head. "It would be too sudden, Charles. Got to let people get used to the idea first."

The ginger Councillor grunted. "Nobody *cares*, Farley. All they care about is who's getting voted off *Strictly Come Dancing*."

"You're wrong, you know," said Topham. He held up a sheet of paper. "This came in yesterday's post. It's a letter from Lisa Seal's brother."

"Who the heck is ..."

"Lisa Seal the *swimmer*," Topham said. "You know – the girl who keeps breaking records, winning medals? They say she could swim for Britain at the next Olympics."

"But what's that got to do with ...?"

"She trains at South Street Baths, it seems," Topham explained. "Twice a day. She's a bit of a hero here in Barton, and her brother's sent a copy of this letter to the *Times*. Her fans might rally round and make trouble if we move too fast."

Ginger Charles thought for a moment. "What if the Baths were *unsafe*, Topham – what then?"

"Well, that would be different," Topham said. "But they're *not* unsafe, are they?"

The other Councillor shrugged. "Nobody knows that, do they? What if an inspector found a weakness – in the roof, say? Think about it. There could be forty kids in the water and suddenly the roof caves in. It would be a disaster. The place has been there a hundred years, after all. I reckon we could get someone to find a weakness – an expert." He winked. "Might cost us a few quid, but nothing like £45,000."

Topham stared at him. "Are you suggesting what I *think* you're suggesting?"

"I am," said Ginger Charles. "I know a man who'd declare the Rock of Gibraltar unsafe if we slipped him three grand." He winked again. "There's more than one way to skin a cat, Councillor."

*

"Nice letter, man," Rick grinned as he dropped the paper on the dinner table in front of Jake.

Jake sat up. "You mean they've *printed* my letter?"

"Not just printed it, man. It's the star letter. It's top of the page in a black frame, which could mean the *Times* is on our side." He laughed. "Councillor Topham will be pig-sick. I wish I could've seen his face when he read it."

"So d'you think we've won, Rick?" Jake's eyes shone.

Rick chuckled. "Nah, man – not yet. They won't cave in *that* easy. We need to keep up the pressure on them."

"How's the protest coming on?" Grandad asked. "People rallying round, are they?"

Rick shrugged. "*Some* people, but not enough yet." He nodded at the paper. "That'll help. It's always good to feel the press is on your side. Doesn't usually happen to guys like us. I'm hoping we'll be ready to go in ten days from now – a week on Saturday. Meanwhile we're putting these out." He pulled a folded leaflet from his pocket and smoothed it out on the table. Everybody leant in to read the large bold type:

DON'T LET CUTS SINK BARTON HERO!

Your Council plans to close the pool where local hero LISA SEAL trains. This will save £180,000 a year – less than one fortieth of the whopping TWO MILLION pounds spent on non-essential renovations of Council offices last year. SOUTH STREET BATHS will close at Christmas, unless the

people of Barton rally round the town's FUTURE OLYMPIC HERO and make their voices heard.

A peaceful march from SOUTH STREET to the TOWN HALL is planned for SATURDAY, SEPTEMBER 14th at 12 noon. EVERYBODY IS WELCOME: THE MORE THE MERRIER.

"Brilliant!" smiled Mum. "How many of these have you got, Rick?'

Rick grinned. "We've given out 2,000 so far. A mate of mine's printing them for nothing. There'll be more when we need 'em."

"*Terrific*!" cried Jake. "Isn't it terrific, Sis? I bet hundreds turn up. *Thousands*."

"Perhaps," Dad nodded, "but you won't be one of them, Jake. Remember what I told you."

"Aw, Dad!"

"It's cool, man," said Rick. "You've done your bit with the letter. It was something else! I bet it hit the Town Hall like a grenade. They'll still be reeling. In fact, you better gimme five."

As Jake's small palm slapped Rick's big one, the Seal family looked at one another and nodded. It was going to be all right.

*

As Jake and Rick high-fived at the Seals' place, Matt Gittins took a swig of his pint and scowled at the mate who'd just joined him in the public bar of The Dog and Gun. "What's up, Vince?" he growled. "You look like someone spat in your drink."

Vince Greaves sneered. "I came 'cause you said it was important, and it turns out all you've got's a leaflet about some poncey march. What's that got to do with me?"

Matt shook his head. "Remember London?" he asked. "Few months back? The riots?"

"Yeah – so?"

"It all started with a march, Vince. A peaceful protest, organised by guys like that tosser Rick Coldwell. Not crims like the papers said." He grinned. "The crims came along later. Joined in. Started smashing stuff up, nicking stuff. The Old Bill waded in, arrested guys, dragged 'em off.

A lot of them were just marchers. Too green to leg it, see? Most of the crims got away, and they took shedloads of gear with them. Flatscreen tellies, iPads, top-of-the-range Rolexes. 'Extreme shopping' it's called. The marchers got the blame. Suited the politicians – took the heat off whatever they'd done that had started the march, see?"

"Whatever." Vincent Greaves yawned. "Who needs the BBC when we've got you to lecture us, Matt?" He drained his glass and stood up.

Matt grabbed the sleeve of his leather jacket. "You don't *get* it do you, you numpty!"

"Get what?"

"This march. Coldwell and his mates can take the rap, and *we* can take the stuff. They'll get their collars felt, we'll get the flatscreen TVs and iPads. Us and a few of our mates. Money for old rope, Vincent old son."

"Ah." A spark of greed lit up in Vincent's eyes. He sat down.

Chapter 5
Professional Reputation

Len Selway ran up the stairs to the phone, sure it would stop ringing before he got to it. He snatched up the handset just in time. "Selway here," he panted.

"Is that Len?"

"Yes it is, who's speaking?"

"Charles. Councillor Lewis."

Selway's heart sank. "What do you want, Councillor?"

"What makes you think I want something?"

Selway saw no need to be polite. "You *always* want something. Last time it was that library – the so-called 'fire hazard'. I put my professional reputation on the line over that one."

"You were well paid for it," the Councillor said. "Now something else has come up."

"I thought it might have," Selway sighed. "What is it? Not that I'm interested, Councillor Lewis. Unless it's straight up, I mean."

"Oh, it's straight up, all right, I'm not a crook, Len. You know we're closing South Street Baths?"

"I read it in the *Times*. Christmas, isn't it?"

"That was the plan, but we might be forced to bring the date forward."

"Oh, and why's that?"

"Health and Safety issues. Well, safety, really. It's the roof. Some of us are afraid it might not last till Christmas. We're not experts, of course, but bits seem to be falling into the water."

"Bits?" Len didn't trust the man, but this did sound bad.

"Yes. Bits of debris. They're turning up in the filters. Flakes of paint, little nuggets of plaster, stuff like that. I've got some here at home, I can show you."

"Why would *I* want to see 'em?" Len asked. "It's nothing to do with me."

"No but it *might* be Len, if you could use three grand, free of tax. All you'd have to do is look at these samples, take a quick peek at the roof itself and confirm our fears. Half an hour's work, a report on headed paper and *kaboom* – there's three thousand smackeroos in your account. The *Times* will tell the people of Barton how a keen-eyed expert spotted a tragedy waiting to happen and saved dozens of innocent lives." There was a pause before Councillor Lewis spoke again. "What d'you say?"

*

"Morning, Marie, morning, Lisa." The pool attendant smiled at the coach and her pupil, sharp as usual that Friday at 7am

"Morning, Sylvia," said Marie. "For someone who'll be out of work by Christmas you're sounding pretty chipper."

Sylvia shrugged. "No point moaning, is there? It'll happen whatever." She pulled a face. "In fact, it might happen even sooner. There's a guy coming at ten today to inspect the roof."

Marie frowned. "What guy?"

"Some man the Council's sending. A structural engineer. I don't know what he's supposed to be looking for, but I don't like the sound of it."

Marie shook her head. "Me neither." She glanced up at the web of Victorian iron-work that held up the glass roof. "It's OK to swim this morning, I suppose?" she asked.

"Oh yeah, it's probably nothing," said Sylvia. "Might be just some jobsworth down the Town Hall panicking. They'd have told me not to open if there was real danger, wouldn't they?"

Marie nodded. "Let's hope so." She looked at Lisa. "Go get changed love, before anything else can go wrong."

As Lisa headed off to change, Sylvia looked at Marie. "Any idea where the two of you'll train after Christmas?"

The coach shook her head. "Haven't a clue." She grinned. "Best would be if some local billionaire with his own pool came forward and offered us free use."

"Oh yeah." Sylvia smiled. "Ten-a-penny in Barton, billionaires. Even better if he could use an attendant for 400 quid a week as well."

"I'll be sure and ask him about that when he contacts me," Marie promised, as Lisa came out in her lycra suit. "In the meantime we'd better get on."

Sylvia nodded. "Work hard, you two. I'm off to put the kettle on while there still is one."

An hour after Marie and Lisa had gone, a ladder came crashing through the swing doors to the pool with a man on each end.

"Whoa!" shouted Sylvia, coming forward with her hands raised. "You can't bring that thing poolside, there's swimmers!"

One of the men frowned. "My name's Selway, you're supposed to be expecting me. Didn't the Council phone?"

Sylvia nodded. "Yes."

"And didn't they tell you to clear the pool?"

"No."

"Idiots." He looked at the other man. "OK, Jim, just lay the ladder along the wall here." To Sylvia he said, "Get everybody out love, we're going to need to move about, down here and up in the roof."

"These people have *paid*," Sylvia protested. "They're entitled to an hour. You can't just ..."

"Tell them the roof's coming down," the man snapped. "They'll be out of that water like penguins near a killer whale."

"But the roof *isn't* coming down."

Selway glared at her. "And how would *you* know, love? Want it on your head if someone gets hurt, do you?"

"Well no, but ..."

"Well, give them their cash back or whatever you need to do, but get them out!"

Sylvia had no choice. A few swimmers grumbled but they all left, with quick peeks up at the roof as they trooped out.

Len Selway poked about for half an hour, clumping up and down the ladder while Jim held it steady. He paused a few times to scribble in a notebook. Sylvia was going to offer them tea but decided not to. They seemed such a pair of miseries.

"How does it look?" she asked as Selway and Jim steered the ladder through a door she held open for them. "*Is* it dangerous, d'you think?"

Selway stared at her. "Paying my fee, are you?"

Sylvia shook her head. "No of course not, but I work here, I just wondered ..."

"I report to whoever pays my fee, love. Your boss'll tell you what you need to know, when you need to know it. Good morning."

Sheila was glad she hadn't offered tea. Once they had gone, she put out the OPEN sign again. An hour later, the phone rang.

"Sylvia Dobson?" the voice on the other end asked. "Jim Grimwith here from Leisure Services. If there's anybody in the building, you must get them out *now*. The roof could fall in at any moment. When everybody's gone, hang out the

CLOSED sign, lock up and go home. You'll be paid up to next Friday, and after that the council will decide what it can offer you, if anything. I'm very sorry. Good morning."

Chapter 6

What's Been Did, What's Been Hid

"Look, Marie: CLOSED." Lisa ran up the three worn steps. The sign hung behind a dusty pane in the door. "She's left us a message." She peered at Sylvia's biro scrawl, read it out as Marie joined her. "*Marie, Lisa – this was even faster than I expected. Sorry. Sylvia.*"

"It's not her fault," Marie growled. "The engineer guy must have found something." She sighed. "I've been thinking all day about what to do if the worst happened. There's only one thing, as far as I can see."

Lisa looked at her. "What's that?"

"Leeds. Once a day, in the afternoon. It's not perfect, just when you need to focus, but it's the best we can do for now."

"No." Lisa shook her head. "It isn't the best, Marie. The best we can do is stop them closing the Baths. Rick is whipping up a lot of support – our big hope is that the demo forces the Council to change its mind."

Marie shook her head. "Don't you see, Lisa? This roof thing scuppers all that. No matter how big the demo, the Council *can't* keep the place open if it's not safe."

Lisa looked stricken. "You mean, the march is no good now? Rick might as well not bother?"

Marie shook her head. "That's how it's turned out, love. I'm sure Rick'll realise when he hears the Baths have closed on safety grounds." She pulled a face. "We're beat, Lisa. Even if we demand the place be repaired, the Council will say there's no dosh to do it with."

"It's not fair." Lisa looked like she was about to cry.

Marie patted her back. “Lots of things aren’t fair, Lisa. People just have to get over it. Come on – we’d better hit your place, tell your mum and dad.”

Lisa got even more worked up on the way home. She almost knocked her mum over as she burst in the door.

“Hello, love,” her Mum said. “You’re early. Nothing wrong I hope?”

Lisa snorted. “Everything!” She threw herself down on the sofa. Marie followed her in and broke the news.

Mum, Jake and Grandad looked stunned. They still looked stunned half an hour later when Dad got home.

“It’s a disgrace,” he growled, when Marie had brought him up to speed. “Why was the place allowed to get into such a state in the first place? Did nobody notice it was ...” He broke off. “Hey – what about the march, the demo? What happens to that now?”

“I’m calling Rick,” Lisa said. “He’ll know what to do – he always does.” She keyed in the number as the others watched.

"Rick, it's me," she said. "They've closed the Baths. They say the roof's not safe. I don't know. Sylvia said some guy was coming – some engineer. She didn't tell me his name. Yes, I've got her home number – what d'you want it for? Oh *right*, I didn't know that. Do you think it was the same guy? So maybe ... yes, I will. Call us back though, won't you – we're all standing here like zombies. Yeah, later." She hung up, turned to the other zombies and smiled.

"I *knew* Rick would know what to do. He's gonna call me back, and I guess in the meantime we can eat." She looked at her mum. "We can feed Marie, can't we?"

"Of course," smiled Mum.

They hadn't finished eating when Rick walked in. Lisa jumped out of her seat. "What've you dug up, Rick?"

Rick chuckled. "Listen to this. The engineer *is* the guy I thought. He condemned Foxton Library last year as a fire hazard – a 'fire trap', he called it. The Council closed it right away, moved everything out. The librarian took early retirement. But the thing is, they still own the building, and get this – a voluntary group is running it as a day centre for people with mobility issues.'"

Lisa shook her head. "Mobility issues? I don't understand – did the Council – you know – alter the place? Make it safe?"

"That's the whole point," said Rick. "They *didn't*. It's exactly as it was."

"So the old folk could be trapped and fried anytime, is that what you're saying?" Dad asked.

"No. What I'm saying is, I don't believe the place is a fire hazard at all. I think it was a scam to close the library. Now, instead of shelling out however many thousands it cost to run it, the Council gets rent from the mobility group."

"Crikey!" Lisa said. "You don't imagine them trying stuff like that, do you? It's *unbelievable*."

Rick laughed. "Case of *what's been did, what's been hid*, sweetheart. Goes on all the time, everywhere. Anyway, listen. Next Saturday's no good to us now. We need to get on this right away, so here's what we do."

They all listened while he explained the plan. He wanted them to phone or text as many people as possible, tell them what had happened, and ask them to be outside the Baths this evening at 8pm. Rick went off to put it up on Facebook, email all the councillors and call the editor of the *Times* at home.

"It won't be the big demo we hoped for," he said, "but people are gonna be mad, so something's bound to kick off."

Once he'd gone, everyone started talking at once.

"It won't work," said Dad. "Not at a couple of hours' notice."

Marie nodded. "You're right, it's too sudden."

"Rubbish!" Grandad bellowed. "Let's shake their windows and rattle their walls, like in the Dylan song."

Jake looked puzzled. "What's a Dylan, Grandad?"

The old man looked at him. "Dylan, lad. Bob Dylan, the most famous protest singer in history. Surely you've heard of ...?"

Jake shook his head. "No, 'cause he's in history like you said."

"I don't want my family arrested," cried Mum, changing the subject. "If that man's a crook it'll come out. We should wait and ..."

"No!" Lisa shook her head. "It's got to be *now*, before they get their excuses lined up. I'm calling a few people, then I'm off to meet up with Rick. You're all invited, but stay if you have to."

"I'm with you Sis!" cried Jake. "And that'll go for Minty, Willie and Garfield too, when I text them. Give me a couple of minutes."

Dad scrambled to his feet. "No, I *told* you Jake. Not you."

"But Dad, if Lisa's going I've got to go, to look after her."

"Look after *me?*" Lisa yelped. "It'll be me looking after *you*, more like." She headed for the door, phone clamped to her ear.

"Oh oh," groaned Marie, starting after her. "It'll be me looking after *both* of you, I think." She turned back as she went out the door. "Sorry, Mr Seal. But I won't let anything bad happen to them."

“Hang on,” Grandad panted, “I’m not as fast as I used to be, but I can still man a barricade if I have to.”

“*Barricade?*” wailed Mum. “Our Jake’s not getting mixed up in any barricades. Jake?” She yelled. “You get back here *now*, d’you hear?” She ran out the door and down the hall, yelling all the way.

In seconds, Dad had the room to himself.

Chapter 7
Nick One, Get One Free

Jake's mum grabbed his arm as they turned onto South Street.

"Geroff," he snarled, jerking himself free. "I'm texting Minty and the others. I thought *you'd* want to support our Lisa as well."

"I *do*!" snapped Mum. "But not like this – not after what happened in London."

"That's got nothing to do with this, Mum," Jake scoffed. "This isn't a riot, it's a march. We're saving South Street Baths, not nicking tellies. Come on – Rick needs as many people as he can get."

"But *look* at me." She spread her arms. "I'm in my joggers! I've got no coat or anything."

"Doesn't *matter*, Mum. Look – we're nearly there."

The Baths were just ahead. People milled about in front of the building. Some held up placards. A new message covered those that had been prepared for next Saturday – WHAT'S BEEN DID, WHAT'S BEEN HID? Rick was on the steps, calling people to order. Jake joined on at the back, craning his neck to see. His mum stood beside him. Marie and Lisa had got down near the front. There was no sign of Grandad.

"Listen up, everyone," Rick said. "Thanks for coming at such short notice. In a minute we'll set off for the Town Hall, but there's a couple of things we need to keep in mind. One, there hasn't been time to tell the police about this march, so it's not totally legal."

"*Stuff* legal," cried a creaky voice in the crowd. Jake grinned. Grandad! His mother shook her head.

"Shutting the Baths wasn't legal either, but they did it anyway!" Grandad shouted.

Rick nodded. "Fair point, Mr Seal, but still. We should stay together, walk in twos down the middle of the road, no breaking away to do our own thing." His eyes searched the crowd till they found Jake. "That goes *double* for you, Jake Seal – your dad'll kill me if you get in any trouble."

That caused a few chuckles in the crowd. "We can chant," Rick said, "but please, no bad language." He smiled, coming down the steps to take Lisa's arm. "OK," he shouted. "Let's do it!"

Even in twos, it wasn't a long line of people. Rick and Lisa took the front, starting a chant which was soon taken up by everyone else.

"*What's been did – what's been hid?*" they called, in time with the tramp of their feet.

There weren't a lot of people out and about, but some stopped to watch. A few shouted words of support as the marchers passed by, and one or two tagged on at the back. As they approached the Shopping Centre they turned up the volume on their chant, lifted their placards higher and put a spring in their step.

*

Matt Gittins had had a bit of a rush as well. In fact, if it hadn't been for his mate Vince, he'd have missed the march altogether. By sheer luck, Vince had walked past the South Street Baths just as the marchers started to gather. He got out his phone and called Matt.

"That march you were on about," he growled. "Looks like they're doing it *now*."

"Wait there," said Matt, "I'll be right with you." He had the things he needed in a sports bag he'd got ready for next Saturday. All he had to do was call a few mates and get his jacket.

"C'mon Tim," he shouted. "It's shopping time."

It was time to bring those stuck-up Seals down a peg or two, and that tosser Rick with them. The brothers headed for the shops.

*

"*What's been did*," bellowed Jake as he strode along beside his mother. "*What's been hid!*"

Jake wasn't sure what the words meant, but they were Rick's words and that was good enough for him. Mum wasn't chanting. She looked a bit fed-up.

By now they'd reached the middle of the Shopping Centre. A couple of community support police officers had shown up but they just kept pace, and made no attempt to interfere with the march. They probably knew that people looking for trouble don't bring along mums in jogging bottoms and old guys walking with sticks. And they didn't notice when a knot of lads in hoodies tagged on at the back, one with a bulky-looking sports bag.

Lisa looked sideways at Rick. "Will there be anyone at the Town Hall?" she asked. "It's nearly 8.30."

Rick grinned. "If you mean councillors, probably not, but that doesn't matter. The *Times* photographer will be there, and maybe someone from *Look North*. That's what counts – the press."

"As long as it's *good* press," Marie put in. "It's no use if ..."

She broke off as a loud crash came from somewhere behind. Rick whirled round. Near the back some people were dashing towards a shop where the large front window lay in pieces on the pavement. At the same time a siren wailed and a police car appeared, with flashing blue lights. The march came to a halt as protestors milled around in confusion.

"Stay together!" Rick yelled. "Our people didn't smash that window, we've done nothing wrong!"

The police car screeched to a halt and three policemen baled out and ran towards the shop.

"Stick together and stand still!" Rick shouted. "That way they can *see* we're not involved!"

Matt Gittins stood in the shattered window, up to his ankles in broken glass and expensive electronics. As the officers ran towards him, he snatched a couple of mobiles off a stand and passed them to his brother.

"Here, kid," he growled. "Plant these on the Seals, then run. I'll catch you later."

Vince Greaves had lifted a sleek flatscreen TV. It was heavy, but he dodged the charging coppers and lugged it towards a marcher. "Here y'are, love!" he laughed. He tipped the set into the woman's arms. "You win tonight's Star Prize."

"Hey, I don't ..." The woman tried to push the TV back at him, but Vincent hurried away. The woman turned, confused, and then lowered the set carefully to the ground. Just then a community police officer gripped her arm.

"Now then, lady," he said. "I hope you're not going to give me any trouble."

Matt's mates were among the marchers now, jeering and throwing half-bricks. Another window exploded, then a third. Guys waded through drifts of glass, helping themselves to shoes, trainers and leather jackets.

Tim Gittins grabbed Jake's arm and swung him round. "Here," he shouted, and thrust the stolen phones at Jake's chest. Jake clutched them without thinking.

"What're you doing?" cried his mother. "We don't want ..."

"Special offer, missus," Tim panted. "Nick one, get one free." He pelted off.

"Drop them, Jake," his mother snapped, "drop them and follow me. We're going home." She turned and set off. Jake didn't want to drop the phones, but he didn't want to get arrested either. He let them fall and rushed off after Mum.

Behind Jake, Matt Gittins skidded into an alley between two shops. He lifted a bottle out of the sports bag, careful not to spill any of the petrol in it. He flicked a disposable lighter and touched the flame to the rag he'd stuffed in the neck. A police van drove by, trying to avoid some guys coming out of The Dog and Gun to get their share of the freebies. Matt hurled the bottle at the van. It struck the visor and covered the windscreen in liquid fire. The crew baled out. Matt slipped away.

Jake's dad met him and his mum halfway home. "I *told* you," he shouted. "I *knew* there would be trouble. It's on TV!" He looked around wildly. "Where's Lisa? You were supposed to be looking after her."

Jake shook his head. "I dunno, Dad! Some hoodies joined on the back, started chucking stuff. Tim Gittins was there, nicking phones."

"Lisa's with Rick," Mum said. "Marie's there too, and Grandad. I'm sure they're looking after her."

Jake wished *he* felt that confident. His sister could be down the police station right now, in a cell, along with Rick and Marie and Grandad. The police might come for Jake and Mum too, any minute.

'Excitement's one thing,' he thought. 'This is something else.'

Chapter 8
Focus

Tim Gittins scowled across the desk at the big police sergeant. "I didn't do nothing," he snapped. "I wasn't even there."

"You heard him," his mum said. "He was at home with me, till your lot dragged him off."

The policeman shook his head. "We got him on video, love. CCTV. Trying to dump the phones he'd nicked on some kid."

"Jake Seal," cried Tim. "I seen him with phones. I didn't dump them on him, he nicked them!"

"How'd you know *that*?" the sergeant asked, "when you weren't even there?"

"You're tricking him," Shelley Gittins screeched. "Getting him confused. It's what you lot do. My boy's innocent."

The policeman leaned forward. "D'you know what I reckon, Mrs Gittins? I reckon your boy planned the whole thing. Bricks, firebombs, the lot. We lost a van tonight, and two of my lads are in the hospital with burns. Your 'innocent boy' is facing three years at least in a Young Offenders' Institution. Not nice. Big rough boys, 16 and 17. They'd kick your face in soon as look at you."

"No." Tim shook his head. There were tears in his eyes. "That's not fair, I didn't plan nothing. It was ..."

The policeman frowned. "It was *who*, lad?"

Tim shook his head. "I'm not a grass."

"Oh, well in that case ... Constable?" The door opened.

"Yes, Sarge?"

"Stick this lad in a cell, will you? I'll talk to him again in the morning."

"No!" Tim looked wildly at his mother. "Mum, don't let them ..." He turned back to the sergeant. "All right, I'll tell you. It was our Matt. He planned it, with Vince Greaves and some mates, to get back at Rick and the Seals. He wanted to get the marchers arrested, like in London." He gulped. "He'll kill me when he gets hold of me."

The sergeant shook his head. "Not if we get hold of him first, he won't." He looked at Shelley. "You might want to wait outside, Madam, while I have a quiet word with your lad here. Then you can take him home."

In fact, the sergeant had a great many words to say to Tim, and none of them was quiet. Tim felt like a lion was roaring in his face. His legs trembled. He tried his best to be hard like his brother, but he was blubbing long before the man stopped shouting. When it was over and he was led out to his mum, he clung to her like a little boy.

*

At the council leader's home, the phone rang. He picked up. "Topham."

"It's Dan Masters, Councillor. From the *Barton Times*, about the South Street Baths."

"It's ten at night, for Heaven's sake!" Topham said. "Can't it wait till tomorrow?"

"I'm afraid not. A guy inspected the Baths this morning, didn't he? Len Selway. Found the building to be unsafe."

"That's correct."

"This is the Len Selway who condemned Foxton Library last year as a fire-trap, right?" the journalist asked.

"Right, but what's ...?"

"The library closed, but it seems that now the Council rents it out as a drop-in centre for disabled people. Just how much of a fire-trap *is* that building, Councillor?"

"I – er – I'm not an expert, Mr Masters. I can't comment."

"You hired Selway, Mr Topham."

"No, I didn't. It was one of my coucillors. He was very concerned and so he arranged it himself."

"But you closed the Baths today, on his word?"

"Not me. Jim Grimwith from Leisure Services did that. You'll have to talk to him, Mr Masters."

"I think you're ducking the issue, Councillor," the journalist said.

Topham snorted. "I don't have to listen to this, I'm hanging up."

"The protestors have given me *their* side of the story, Councillor. Don't you want to give yours?"

"Protestors? Bunch of thieves, more like."

"What's been did, councillor," said the reporter. "What's been hid. Hello ...?"

The line was dead.

*

Thanks to Tim Gittins (or Gittins the Grass, as his brother called him), the cops didn't come for Jake. They didn't come for Lisa either, or Grandad, or Rick. They came for Matt Gittins and most of his mates, and left the protestors alone.

On Wednesday the *Barton Times* ran a piece by Dan Masters that caused a certain ginger-haired councillor to resign. And when Masters called to quiz Len Selway on the two buildings he'd condemned, it turned out the engineer had been called away on urgent business. Nobody seemed to know when he'd be back.

It took Farley Topham several days to get on top of the panic at the Town Hall. The *Times* kept up the pressure, and after two weeks the council was forced to reopen the South Street Baths.

In a speech on local radio, Topham said the Baths had been closed due to a mistake in the paperwork. Listening to this over fish and chips on Wednesday, Rich and the Seals jumped about whooping. It sounded like they'd won.

They hadn't. Topham hadn't finished.

"The re-opening," he said, "is temporary. At Christmas the Baths will close for good as part of the cuts, as we decided in the first place."

The whooping stopped. The Seals looked at one another. A tear trickled down Lisa's cheek. "So that's it," she choked. "Next year, no place to train. No way to *focus*. No gold medal. No Olympics."

"I'm sorry, love," said Dad. He put his arm round her. "After all your years of hard work. It's really rotten luck."

The others gathered round, murmuring how sorry they were.

"You'd have won gold, Sis," Jake said. "Everyone *knows* you would."

"Yes," said Mum. "And you'll get straight A's in your A-levels. They can't take that away."

"Unless they close the school as well," muttered Grandad. "Save a bit more money."

The phone rang. When nobody else moved to answer it, Rick picked up. "Oh, hi," he said. "We've just been listening to that crook Topha– *What*? Who did? When was this?"

Everybody stopped talking to watch him. Who *was* he talking to? He was smiling and laughing. After a bit he said, "It's a big ask, Marie, but we'll give it our best shot, won't we?" He hung up and turned to the Seals, eyes shining.

"That was Marie," he said. "Somebody's just phoned her, said if we can get a bunch of people together and give ourselves a name, such as *Friends of South Street Baths*, we can apply to the

Heritage Lottery Fund for dosh to buy the Baths from the council and run them ourselves."

Lisa's mouth fell open. "Oh wow!" she breathed. "Do you really think we could?"

Rick held up his hands. "Don't see why not. Other people have done it."

Jake pulled a face. "Rotten name though, *Friends of South Street Baths*. How about *Focus*?"

Rick looked at him. "Nice one, kid," he smiled. "Toss me a chip willya – I'm a hungry man."

Our books are tested
for children and young people by
children and young people.

Thanks to everyone who consulted on
a manuscript for their time and effort in
helping us to make our books better
for our readers.

Also by **Robert Swindells...**

Dan's War

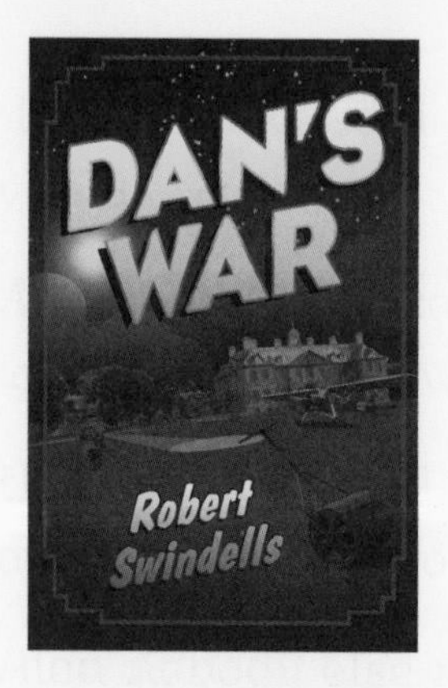

World War Two

Dan dreams of going off to fight. But he has his mother to think of. Digging the gardens at Winton Hall might be boring, but at least it pays.

But then Dan notices something odd at the Hall. The General may not be all he seems.

Can Dan find out the truth before it's too late?

Just a Bit of Fun

Halloween

Harley's got to take his little brother and sister trick-or-treating. Then, when Harley's not looking, they go missing. And when he finds them, something's happened.

They're different. They want to play. But there are no rules to this game...